CARTOON
NETWORK™

SCOOBY-DOO!™

AND THE
FAIRGROUND PHANTOM

Look for the **Scooby-Doo Mysteries**.
Collect them all!

Coming soon:

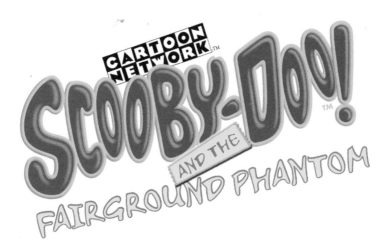

Written by
James Gelsey

A
LITTLE APPLE
PAPERBACK

SCHOLASTIC INC.
New York Toronto London Auckland Sydney
Mexico City New Delhi Hong Kong

ISBN 0-439-10664-8

12 11 10 9 8 7 6 5 4 3 2   0 1 2 3 4 5 6/0

Special thanks to Duendes Del Sur for cover and interior illustrations.
Printed in the U.S.A.
First Scholastic printing, May 2000

For Chuck and Sheri

SCOOBY-DOO!™

AND THE FAIRGROUND PHANTOM

"Hey, Fred!" Shaggy called from the back of the Mystery Machine. "Why'd we stop?"

"We're stuck in traffic," Fred replied. "It looks like all these cars are headed to the same place."

"Like, where's that?" Shaggy asked.

"Todey Fields," Daphne answered. "You know, for the county fair."

"The fair's in a field full of frogs?" Shaggy said.

"Reeeecccchhhh," Scooby barked. "Ri rate rogs!"

"Me too, Scoob," Shaggy agreed. "All they

1

do is jump around everywhere and make that croaking sound."

"Reah." Scooby nodded his head up and down. "Rike ris." Scooby started hopping around the back of the Mystery Machine like a frog.

"Ribbit, ribbit," Scooby barked. He and Shaggy started laughing.

"What are you two doing back there?" Velma asked.

"Like, being frogs, like Daphne said," Shaggy explained.

"I didn't say anything about frogs," Daphne said.

"Sure you did, Daph," Shaggy said. "You said we were almost at Froggy Fields."

"I said *Todey* Fields," Daphne said.

"Toads, frogs, same difference," Shaggy replied.

"No, Shaggy, it's not toady, like in frogs," Velma explained. "It's Todey, spelled T-o-d-e-y. As in General Sherwin Todey."

"Like, I don't suppose he was a frog?" Shaggy asked.

"No, he was a Revolutionary War hero," Velma continued. "He fought off the redcoats and helped win the war. His most famous victory happened where the county fair is being held. That's why they call it Todey Fields."

"So, like, there aren't any frogs there?" Shaggy said.

"No frogs, Shaggy," Daphne said.

"But they are going to have a really cool show where people will act out General Todey's famous battle," Fred said. "People will be dressed in Revolutionary War costumes and everything."

"But Scooby-Doo and I are going to have

a really cool show of our own," Shaggy said.

"What kind of show?" Daphne asked.

"A show where we'll act out eating lunch!" Shaggy replied.

"Reah, runch," barked Scooby.

"You know, there's more to the fair than just food," Velma said.

"Velma's right," Daphne agreed. "There are craft exhibits, pie-baking contests, livestock shows, not to mention —"

Shaggy and Scooby perked up. "Hold on there, Daphne," Shaggy interrupted. "Did you say pie-baking contests?"

Daphne nodded.

"Scooby-Doo," Shaggy said, "we've found the answer to our prayers. Imagine eating as many pies as you possibly can. Like, how come we don't come to the county fair more often?"

"Because they only hold it once a year," Fred explained. He steered the Mystery Machine through the parking gate and pulled into a parking space.

"Well, here we are, gang," Fred said. "It's time to visit the county fair."

Chapter 2

The gang walked through the parking lot to the front gate. Giant COUNTY FAIR flags waved in the wind. The gang bought their tickets and walked through the gate.

They saw a huge banner hanging on the side of a building. It was a picture of a man riding a horse. The man was wearing an old military uniform.

"That must be General Sherwin Todey," Velma said.

"You're right!" a man called. The gang looked over and saw a man sitting behind a table. A SAVE TODEY FIELDS sign leaned against

6

the front of the table. The man waved at the gang. The gang walked over.

"You're the first person all day to recognize the picture of General Todey," he said.

"It does seem kind of obvious," Velma said. "After all, we are at Todey Fields."

"You're the first person all day to know that, too," the man added sadly. "I'm Ben Crenshaw."

"Nice to meet you," Fred said. "Do you work for the fair?"

"Yes," Ben said. "I'm a Revolutionary War buff. I know a lot about General Todey in particular. So they asked me to research and put together the part of the show where they do the battle. I even get to play General Todey."

"You don't sound so happy about it," Daphne commented.

"I am, sort of," Ben replied. "You see, it's really important to me that people learn about General Todey. The problem is that the fair is right on top of the battlefield. There are tons of artifacts buried here. But the people who run the fair won't let me do any digging. And as long as the fair keeps coming back here, it will continue to ruin the land. Soon there won't be anything left worth looking for."

"Except old snow-cone cups and peanut shells," a man behind them said. Everyone turned and saw a man in a blue suit. His hair was combed straight back and he had a pencil-thin moustache.

"I'm Clarence Sims," the man said. "Pleased to meet you."

"Are you the same Clarence Sims who owns the chain of Sims gas stations?" Velma asked.

"Yes," Clarence replied. "And I happen to agree with Mr. Crenshaw. The fair is ruining this land."

"You agree with me?" Ben asked. "Then let's do something about it!"

9

"Not so fast," Clarence added. "This land is valuable because of its prime location. I've been trying to get my hands on it for some time now. And when I do, it certainly won't be to dig it up looking for old bullets."

"Now wait just a minute, Mr. Sims," Ben began.

The gang stepped back as Ben Crenshaw and Clarence Sims started arguing.

"What do you say we check out the rest of the fair before it's time for the show?" Fred suggested.

"Good idea," Daphne replied. "Let's go."

"Like, Scooby and I are starting to get a little hungry," Shaggy said.

"Let's start walking around together and see if we come across any food," Velma said. "That way we can keep an eye on you two."

"Like, what for?" Shaggy asked. "It's not like we can cause any trouble at a fair."

"We don't want to take any chances," Daphne replied. "Let's go."

Chapter 3

The gang followed a path to a bright orange tent. Inside, rows of handmade quilts were hanging on clotheslines.

"Hey, check out those blankets, Scoob," Shaggy said. "They look just like giant square pizzas with everything on it."

"Why, I've never heard quilts compared to pizzas before," a woman said. "You must be very hungry."

The gang turned and saw a woman with blonde hair standing next to them.

"Hi, I'm Alice Atchinson," she said. "I run the fair."

"Pleased to meet you," Daphne replied.

"Are you having a good time?" Alice asked.

"I'd say so," Fred said. "Though we haven't been able to do much yet."

Suddenly, someone yelled, "ALICE ATCHINSON!"

Alice rolled her eyes. "Oh, no," she sighed.

A short woman wearing a bright pink apron ran up to Alice and the gang.

"There you are, Alice," the woman said. "I've been looking for you. How could you disqualify me from the baking contest?"

"Heddy, you're a professional pie chef," Alice said. "You own a bakery in town. It's not fair for you to compete against regular people."

"You just made up that rule to keep me out," Heddy complained. "Just because I won the contest the past five years in a row."

"That's not true, Heddy," Alice replied.

"If that's the way you want to be about it, fine," Heddy said. "You won't have to worry about Heddy Blocker entering any more baking contests. And you can also forget about me judging the apple pie finals. I'm warning you, Alice, I won't forget this!"

Heddy Blocker turned and walked away. Alice Atchinson just shook her head.

"Jinkies, she was mad," Velma said.

"I just hope she doesn't do anything foolish," Alice said. "The last thing the fair needs now is more bad publicity."

"What do you mean?" Fred asked.

"Ben Crenshaw's been trying to get the county to move the fair so he can dig up some artifacts," Alice explained. "And then there's Clarence Sims, who wants to buy the land for his own purposes. If one more thing goes wrong, I'm afraid we'll lose the field and the fair will close down for good."

"Like, that's too bad," Shaggy said. "But look on the bright side. Scooby-Doo and I can help judge the pie contest."

"Shaggy!" Daphne scolded. "Ms. Atchinson has more important things to worry about right now."

"Oh, that's all right," Alice said. "It's very kind of him to offer. And it would help me out on such short notice. It will be my pleasure to let them judge the contest. Here you go."

Alice reached into her pocket and took out two small blue ribbons. The ribbons had the words OFFICIAL JUDGE written on them.

"Didja hear that, Scooby-Doo?" Shaggy said. "We're going to judge the apple pie contest. A dream come true. Thanks, Ms. Atchinson."

"Reah, ranks!" Scooby barked. He jumped up and gave Alice a lick on her cheek.

"You're welcome," Alice said, smiling. "The contest is about to begin. It's in the next tent. Just go on in and they'll send you to the judges' table. Have fun!"

"And be careful!" Velma added.

"What do you mean?" Shaggy asked. "We're just going to eat — I mean judge — some apple pies. What could we possibly do?"

"I don't want to find out," Velma replied. "We'll meet you afterward at the outdoor stage."

Chapter 4

Shaggy and Scooby ran over to the next tent. They adjusted their official blue judges' ribbons and walked inside. Shaggy and Scooby raised their heads and took a big sniff.

"Mmmmmmmm," Scooby said.

"Mmmmmmmm," Shaggy echoed. "It smells like a cake just came out of the oven."

One of the baking contest officials walked over. She was wearing a red ribbon that said COUNTY FAIR OFFICIAL.

"Are you here for the pie contest?" she asked.

18

"Like, right-a-rooney," Shaggy replied.

"Splendid! I'm Gertie Gump. I'm in charge of the contest. Right this way," Gertie said. She turned and walked over to a long table draped with a red and white tablecloth. Shaggy and Scooby followed.

"Please, have a seat right here," Gertie said. Shaggy and Scooby each sat on a folding chair behind the table.

"Here's how we'll do it," Gertie said. "We'll put a plate in front of each of you. You'll each take a bite and then write down a score to rate the pie. Then, after you've tasted them all, you'll talk it over and announce the winner. Are you ready?"

"Ready!" Scooby barked.

"Like, ready." Shaggy nodded.

"Then here we go," Gertie said. She placed a slice of pie in front of Shaggy and Scooby. Shaggy and Scooby smiled as they picked up their forks and put some pie into their mouths. As they chewed the pie, their smiles turned to frowns and their frowns to yuck faces.

"Like, this is the worst apple pie I've ever tasted," Shaggy said.

"That's because they're not apple pies," Gertie said. "They're turnip pies. The apple pie contest is on the other side of the tent."

Shaggy and Scooby looked at each other.

"Rurnip ries?" Scooby asked. He turned a little green in the face and let out a small burp. "Recccchhhhh."

"I'm with you, Scooby-Doo," Shaggy said. "Turnips are definitely not where it's at. Like, let's get out of here before they make us taste cabbage cookies."

When Shaggy and Scooby stood up to leave, someone rode into the tent on horseback. The horse was white as a ghost. The man was dressed in some kind of old military uniform.

"Zoinks!" Shaggy exclaimed. "It's a ghost!" He and Scooby dived under the table.

"Hear me now!" the ghost said. "I am the ghost of General Sherwin Todey. I have come to warn you to leave this place at once and never return. Anyone who remains will be cursed to haunt Todey Fields by my side for all eternity!"

The ghostly man rode out on his horse just as quickly as he entered. Everyone in the tent was in shock until someone screamed. Then everyone started running out of the tent.

Shaggy peeked out from under the tablecloth. "It looks like he's gone, Scoob," Shaggy said. "Let's go find the others." He and Scooby jumped out from under the table and ran out of the tent.

Chapter 5

Shaggy and Scooby ran in and out of tents until they found their way to the outdoor stage. They searched the crowd and finally found Fred, Daphne, and Velma.

"Hey, how did the judging go?" Fred asked. "Did you get your fill of pies?"

"No, but we got our fill of ghosts," Shaggy answered.

"What are you talking about?" Daphne asked.

"Like, the ghost of General Todey came to the tent," Shaggy said.

"I'll bet he wanted a piece of apple pie," Fred joked.

"After he scared everyone away," Shaggy said. "He could have had all the pies!"

"Shaggy, I'm sure it was only Ben Crenshaw getting into character for the battle scene," Velma explained. "He probably scared everyone out of the tent so they'd come to the stage and see the show."

"I don't know, Velma," Shaggy said. "He seemed pretty hot under the collar, right, Scoob?"

"Reah." Scooby nodded. "Rike ris." Scooby stood up on his back legs. He wildly waved his front paws and growled.

"Would you two just forget about that and

calm down?" Daphne asked. "The show's starting."

The gang sat down on the benches. The lights lit up the stage.

"Like, wow, Scoob," Shaggy said. "We should have gotten some popcorn for the show."

"Reah," Scooby sighed.

"Shhh . . ." Velma said as the music started.

The actors walked to different places on the stage and stood still. Some were dressed like American colonists and some in the red coats of the British army. Then Alice Atchinson walked out on stage.

"Good afternoon, ladies and gentlemen," she began. "Thank you for coming to the historic play of the battle of Todey Fields. It is 1776 and the British soldiers are battling the colonial army."

Just then, the ghostly General Todey rode out onto the stage on his ghostly horse.

"Zoinks!" Shaggy cried. "It's him! The ghost!"

"Jinkies!" Velma said.

"Wow," Daphne and Fred said at the same time.

The ghost of General Todey turned to the audience. "I warn all of you to leave this cursed battleground immediately and for all time," he yelled. "If you do not obey me, you will be cursed to haunt this field forever, like so!"

General Todey threw something at Alice Atchinson. There was a flash of light and smoke. And when the smoke cleared, Alice was as white as General Todey.

"Jinkies," Velma said. "He really turned her into a ghost!"

General Todey turned his horse around. As he galloped off, he reached down and scooped up the ghostly Alice Atchinson. Everyone in the audience screamed and ran out. Fred turned to the others.

"Gang, it looks like we've got a mystery to solve," he said.

"I was afraid you were going to say that," Shaggy moaned.

"Let's split up to look for clues," Fred said. "Daphne and I will check things out around the stage."

"Good idea, Fred," Velma said. "I'll take Shaggy and Scooby back to the place where they first saw the ghost. Let's meet back here as soon as we can."

Chapter 6

Velma, Shaggy, and Scooby walked back through the fairground to the baking tent.

"How is it that you two always manage to be the first ones to find trouble?" Velma asked.

"Like, we don't find trouble," Shaggy replied. "It finds us."

Inside the tent, Velma looked around.

"So where did General Todey come in from?" she asked.

"Over there," Shaggy said. He pointed to the opening on the far side of the tent.

"Ruh-uh," Scooby barked. "Rover rere." He pointed to an opening on the other side of the tent.

"Now look, Scoob, we were sitting over there eating turnip surprise," Shaggy said. "And then the galloping ghost came in. Remember?"

Scooby shook his head and pointed to the other side of the tent.

Velma noticed something on the ground.

"While you two are arguing, I'm going to check something out," Velma said. She walked through one of the openings in the tent.

Shaggy and Scooby continued to argue.

"Like, I'm telling you for the last time, Scoob," Shaggy insisted. "He came in over there."

"I think Scooby was right," Velma called from outside the tent.

"Like, how do you know?" Shaggy asked.

"Call it a ghostly guess," Velma responded. She walked back into the tent looking white as a ghost.

"Zoinks!" Shaggy exclaimed. "Velma's a ghost! General Todey got her!"

"Rikes!" Scooby barked as he jumped into Shaggy's arms.

Velma folded her arms. "Would you two

cut it out?" she said. "I'm not a ghost. Come with me and I'll show you."

Velma turned and walked back through the opening in the tent. Shaggy and Scooby followed her. They walked behind a large bush.

"Here's your ghost maker," Velma said. She pointed to an enormous open bag of flour leaning against the bush. "Whoever turned Alice Atchinson into a ghost just covered her with flour."

"Boy, Velma, add a few eggs and a cup of sugar and you could be a cookie," Shaggy said.

Scooby licked his lips. "Mmmmmm," he said.

"Knock it off, you two," Velma said. "We still need to find more clues if we're going to solve this mystery. Let's go see what Fred and Daphne found."

Velma, Shaggy, and Scooby walked back through the tent. Velma continued, but Shaggy and Scooby stopped just before leaving the tent.

"Like, do you see what I see?" Shaggy asked.

"Ruh-huh," Scooby replied.

Off to one side they saw a long table. On it sat plates of cookies, cakes, and pies.

"These must be things for the baking contests," Shaggy guessed. "It would be a shame

to let them go to waste. What do you say we have a contest of our own, Scoob?"

"Reah!" Scooby barked happily. He and Shaggy walked over to the table of baked goods.

There were so many choices. Scooby and Shaggy didn't know what to eat first.

"So much food and so little time," Shaggy sighed. "Let's dig in!"

Shaggy and Scooby each took a handful of cookies.

"These look like award-winning cookies to me," Shaggy said.

"Oh reah," Scooby said.

Just as they were about to chow down, General Todey jumped up from behind the table. He stood up tall and looked angry.

"I warned you!" General Todey yelled. "I warned you to stay away from this battle-ground!"

He galloped toward Shaggy and Scooby on his ghostly white horse.

"Rikes!" Scooby yelled. "The rhost! The rhost!"

Scooby and Shaggy tossed their cookies into the air and ran out of the tent.

Chapter 7

Shaggy and Scooby ran as fast as they could back to the outdoor stage.

"Make way!" Shaggy shouted. "There's a ghost coming our way!" He and Scooby ran right past Velma, Fred, and Daphne.

"Like, that was them," Shaggy called. "Put on the brakes, Scoob!" Shaggy and Scooby came to a screeching halt. They turned around and ran back to the others.

"Don't just stand there," Shaggy said. "Scooby and I just saw the ghost again and he's really mad. We'd better get out of here."

"Just a minute, Shaggy," Daphne said. She

turned back to Velma. "So the ghost used flour to make himself and Alice Atchinson look so ghostly?"

"Exactly." Velma nodded. "It looks like our ghost is pretty clever."

"Clever, but clumsy," Fred added. "Take a look at what Daphne and I found backstage."

Fred held out two pieces of paper.

"Like, that's nothing but a schedule and map of the fair," Shaggy said. "What's so special about it?"

"Someone circled the time and location of the historic play in red pen," Daphne replied. "Someone did not want to miss it."

"Jinkies," Velma said as she looked at the other paper. "This map looks like it's a couple hundred years old."

"But what are those black triangles all over it?" Daphne asked.

"If I'm not mistaken," Velma said, "they're the answer to our mystery."

"Velma's right," Fred agreed. "The ghost of General Todey has made his last stand. Now it's time to set a trap."

"Uh, Scooby and I just remembered we forgot to do something," Shaggy said.

"What?" Daphne asked.

"Like, stay in bed this morning," Shaggy answered. "Let's go back to the quilt display and hit the hay, Scoob."

"Right!" Scooby barked as he and Shaggy started walking away.

"Not so fast, you two," Velma called.

"We're going to need your help to catch the ghost."

"I knew you'd say that," Shaggy said.

"This ghost won't go away until he's convinced that everyone's left the fairground," Fred said. "So it's up to us to make him think that we're not going anywhere."

"Fred, let me see that schedule again," Velma asked. She looked at the schedule for a moment and smiled.

"There's only one event left for the day," Velma said. She looked at Scooby and smiled. "Shaggy and Scooby-Doo, have we got a job for you."

"Ruh-uh," Scooby said, shaking his head.

"Are you sure?" Velma asked.

"Rup," Scooby replied.

"Then I guess we'll have to get someone else to participate in the all-you-can-eat pie-eating contest," Velma said.

"Rie-eating rontest?" Scooby asked. He started wagging his tail.

"Remember, Scoob," Shaggy warned, "there's a ghost."

"Rooooh, a rhost," Scooby said. "Rorget rit."

"I can't believe I'm saying this," Velma said. "But you can have one Scooby Snack now and all the pie you can eat later."

"Rokay!" Scooby barked. He jumped into the air and gobbled down the Scooby Snack.

"We don't have much time, gang," Fred said. "So let's get to work!"

Chapter 8

Everyone returned to the baking contest tent. Shaggy and Scooby sat on the folding chairs behind the long table. Daphne and Velma stacked up pies on the table.

"Shaggy, Daphne and I need to borrow your blue judges' ribbons," Velma said. Shaggy and Scooby gave their ribbons to Velma and Daphne.

"I'll hide behind that big banner next to the table," Fred explained. "When the ghost comes in, I'll give the signal. Shaggy and Scooby, you grab the ghost. I'll come out and throw the banner over him." Fred stepped behind the banner.

Velma and Daphne stood off to the side and pretended to judge.

"Ready, fellas?" Daphne asked.

"Ready!" Scooby barked. He stared at the pile of pies and licked his lips.

"On your mark," Velma called. "Get set. Go!"

Shaggy and Scooby started munching on the pies. Shaggy picked up one pie at a time and took a bunch of bites. Scooby piled three pies on top of one another. He held them in his paw like a sandwich and took a big bite.

Suddenly, General Todey burst in from the far side of the tent.

"I warned you people," he bellowed as he

ran toward Shaggy and Scooby. "I warned you to leave this cursed place! Now you shall be cursed to haunt these grounds for all eternity!"

General Todey raised his arm and prepared to throw something at Shaggy and Scooby. Before he could, Shaggy stood up and threw a pie at General Todey.

SPLAT! It hit him right in the face. General Todey dropped what he was holding. A huge cloud of white flour filled the tent.

"Now, fellas, grab him!" Fred called. He jumped out from behind the banner and

yanked it down. Then he ran into the cloud of flour.

"Like, I can't see him with all this white stuff in the air," Shaggy said as he ran into the giant cloud.

"Got him!" Fred called. The white flour slowly started clearing.

"Like, you got me," Shaggy yelled from under the banner. Fred helped Shaggy out from the banner.

"If I got you," Fred began, "then where's the ghost?"

Shaggy looked around. "Like, over there!" he yelled. "Behind you, Scooby-Doo!"

Scooby turned and saw the ghost of General Todey standing right behind him.

"Rikes!" Scooby barked.

"Arrrrrrrggghhhh," the ghost yelled.

The ghost reached out to grab Scooby. Scooby jumped up to run away but his tail got caught in the folding chair. Scooby ran toward the other side of the tent, dragging the chair. The ghost of General Todey was right behind him. Fred and Shaggy ran after General Todey, trying to catch him.

The chair slipped off Scooby's tail as he ran out of the tent. Fred and Shaggy threw the banner into the air to catch the ghost. But General Todey tripped on the chair and landed on the long table full of leftover baked goods instead.

"Oh, man," Shaggy sighed. "What a waste of some perfectly good snacks."

General Todey got up and chased after Scooby. Scooby ran into the quilting tent.

Scooby looked over his shoulder and saw General Todey close behind. He turned and saw he was about to run right into a giant quilt. At the last moment, Scooby ducked out of the way. General Todey couldn't stop and got all tangled up in the quilt. He crashed right into one of the tent poles and fell to the ground.

red and Shaggy ran over and held General Todey tightly. Velma showed up with Alice Atchinson.

"Look, Fred, it's the ghost of the lady who runs the fair!" Shaggy exclaimed.

"She's not a ghost, Shaggy," Velma said. "It's really Alice Atchinson."

"Where'd you find her?" Fred asked.

"Right after General Todey ran in, I noticed something fall out of his pocket," Velma said. "It was a key ring. Real ghosts don't need keys to get into places. So Daphne and I went to check the stage area again, where Alice disappeared. One of the keys unlocked the shed behind the stage."

"The ghost locked me up in there after he took me from the stage," Alice explained. "I think someone else was locked in there somewhere, too."

"Daphne stayed to check it out," Velma said. "Now, would you like to see who this mysterious ghost really is, Ms. Atchinson?"

"You bet," Alice said. "I can't wait." She reached over and removed the general's mask.

"Clarence Sims!" Alice exclaimed.

"Just as we suspected," Velma said.

"Though not at first," Fred added.

"Our first suspect was actually Heddy Blocker."

"Heddy? How come?" Alice asked.

"First, she didn't make any secret about wanting to get back at you for keeping her out of the contest," Velma explained. "Plus, as a baker, she'd have access to all that flour."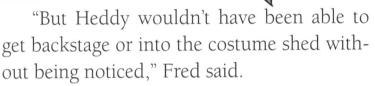

"But Heddy wouldn't have been able to get backstage or into the costume shed without being noticed," Fred said.

"That's why our next suspect was Ben Crenshaw," Velma said. "He helped put the whole battle scene together. That means he could walk around backstage without any problem."

"Like, then why would he need a map and schedule to tell him when and where he needed to be?" Shaggy asked.

"I wouldn't," Ben replied. He walked into

the quilting tent with Daphne and some policemen. "I also wouldn't want the memory of General Todey to be associated with bad things."

"Where'd you come from?" Shaggy asked.

"I found him locked in the costume trunk in the shed," Daphne said.

"Why would you go through all this, Clarence?" Alice asked.

"Maybe this map can help explain," Fred said. He showed everyone the map with the black triangles on it.

"You found my map!" Clarence exclaimed. "I needed that map. It shows all the places on this land where there are underground oil wells. I kidnapped Ben to get his General Todey costume. Then I pretended to turn Alice into a ghost in order to scare everyone away. Once the fair closed down, I was going to buy the land and drill for oil. That way I could expand my chain of gas stations across the country. And I would've gotten away with everything, if it weren't for those meddling kids and their pesky dog."

Ben Crenshaw looked at the old map.

"It looks like the joke's on you, Clarence," Ben said.

"What are you talking about?" Clarence asked. "That's a genuine map. I had it checked out by an antiques dealer."

51

"Oh, the map is real," Ben continued. "But these triangles don't mean oil. In fact, they don't mean anything. This is a decoy map that General Todey himself drew to prepare for his famous battle. He drew the triangles to represent secret treasure. He knew the British soldiers would come to get the treasure. That's how he won the battle."

"Looks like General Todey even outsmarted you, too," Alice said.

"Blast that General Todey!" Clarence yelled as the policemen took him away.

"I can't thank you kids enough," Alice said. "You saved me. You saved Ben. You saved the whole fair. You're our hero, Scooby-Doo."

"Awww, rorget rit," Scooby said as he blushed.

"I want to do something special for you," Alice said. "And I have the perfect idea."

The next day, the fair reopened. Scooby

sat up front for the battle scene. Ben Crenshaw came on stage as General Todey. He and the colonial army defeated the British soldiers. At the end of the battle, Ben marched across the stage carrying a flag with Scooby's image sewn onto it.

"Hooray for the U.S.A.!" Ben shouted. "And hooray for Scooby-Doo!"

"Scooby-Dooby-Doo!" barked Scooby proudly.

About the Author

As a boy, James Gelsey used to run home from school to watch the Scooby-Doo cartoons on television (only after finishing his homework). Today, he still enjoys watching them with his wife and two daughters. He also has a real dog named Scooby who loves nothing more than a good Scooby Snack!